Bucket L
Couples

444
Date Ideas to create Memories

This bucket list belongs:

. . . . & . . . .

Your best photo together

the best
Couple since:

D: . . . .

Table of contents

Foreword

Love must be rediscovered every day.

Every day together is precious and it is worth savoring every moment together. Love demands trust and constancy as well as surprises and new experiences.

Shared experiences and memories strengthen a relationship in a very special way. Let yourself be guided by the inspiration in this book and see how your relationship will grow. This bucket list for couples is not just a collection of experiences, but a declaration of love for the time together and the little moments that will strengthen the bond between you.

Social commitment:

☑ __Wwoofing:__
Works on an organic farm (wwoofing)

☑ __Night flea market:__
Run your own stand at a night flea market

☑ __Donate blood:__
Go donate blood for a good cause

☑ __Guerilla Garding:__
Guerilla Garding - Plant a beautiful plant in your city

☑ __Nature garbage:__
Cleans up a littered place in nature

☑ __Voluntary work:__
Volunteer together (soup kitchen, animal shelter, etc.)

☑ __Act of kindness:__
Makes a random act of kindness

☑ __Demonstrate:__
Demonstrate together for something

☑ __Bone marrow donor:__
Register as a bone marrow donor

☑ <u>Adopt a child:</u>
Give a child a chance

☑ <u>Heart's desire:</u>
Fulfill a loved one's heart's desire

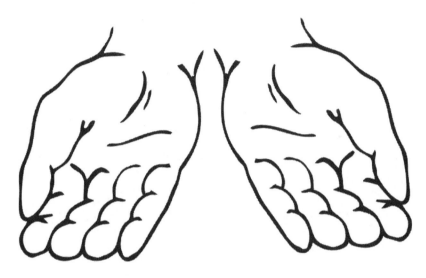

☑ <u>Plant a tree:</u>
Plant a tree together

☑ <u>Rainforest:</u>
Buy a piece of rainforest

☑ <u>Plastic:</u>
Collecting plastic on a littered beach

☑ <u>Food:</u>
Buy a homeless person something to eat

☑ <u>Animal shelter:</u>

Adopt an animal from an animal shelter

☑ <u>Electric car:</u>

Only drive an electric car in future

☑ <u>Children's home donation</u>

Donate something to a children's home (clothes, toys, etc.)

Spirituality:

☑ **Beach ride:**
Rides along the beach on a horse

☑ **Floating:**
Floating - Let yourself drift

☑ **Loneliness:**
Enjoy solitude in a remote location

☑ **Fishing:**
Enjoy the peace and quiet while fishing

☑ **Tea ceremony:**
Take part in a tea ceremony

☑ **Esoteric fair:**
Visit an esoteric fair

☑ **Sunrise Sunset:**
Observe the sunrise and sunset in one day

☑ **River bike tour:**
Go on a day trip by bike along a major river

☑ **Hot coals:**
Walk over hot coals

☑ <u>24 hours of silence:</u>
Silent for 24 hours

☑ <u>Bird watching:</u>
Birding - Observe rare birds

☑ <u>Name star:</u>
Buy a star and give it a name

☑ <u>Observe the stars:</u>
Observe the stars with a telescope

☑ <u>Fortune teller:</u>
Goes to a fortune teller

☑ <u>Cloverleaf:</u>
Finds a four-leaf clover

☑ <u>Incense ceremony</u>
Take part in an incense ceremony

Financial experiments and goals

✓ <u>Lotto:</u>
Play the lottery together

✓ <u>Passive income:</u>
Build up a passive income

✓ <u>Build a business:</u>
Build a business together

✓ <u>Puzzle competition:</u>
Solve a puzzle together and take part in the competition
✓ <u>Quiz show</u>

Take part in a quiz show on television

✓ <u>Poker tournament:</u>
Take part in a poker tournament

✓ <u>Casino:</u>
Visit a casino

✓ <u>Metal detector:</u>
Go on a treasure hunt with a metal detector

✓ <u>Foreclosure:</u>
Take part in a forced sale of real estate

✓ <u>Salary increase</u>
Ask your bosses for a pay rise

✓ <u>Working abroad</u>
Work in a foreign country where there is a higher salary

Childhood

Dance summer rain:
Dancing in the warm summer rain

Twister:
Play Twister with friends

Children's playground:
Let off steam in a children's playground

Sandcastle:
Build a sandcastle together

Ring the bell:
Makes a ringing prank

Ferris wheel:
Ride on a Ferris wheel (in London)

Bumper cars:
Ride on a bumper car

Water sprinkler:
Run through a water sprinkler

Water park:
Visit a water park

Scavenger hunt:
Take part in a scavenger hunt

☑ A visit home:
Visit your respective childhood homes

Indoor playground:
Visit an indoor playground

Health

☑   **<u>Wellness Spa:</u>**
Treat yourself to a day at a wellness spa

☑   **<u>Thermal bath:</u>**
Treat yourself to a day in a thermal spa

☑   **<u>Herb hike:</u>**
Take part in a herb hike

☑   **<u>Wellness day at home:</u>**
Create a wellness day at home

☑   **<u>Hamam:</u>**
Spend an afternoon in a hammam

☑   **<u>Ice bathing:</u>**
Goes ice swimming in winter

☑   **<u>New Year's swimming:</u>**
Plunge into the ice-cold waters at the New Year's swim

☑   **<u>Salt cave:</u>**
Relax in a salt cave

☑   **<u>Detox cure:</u>**
Go on a detox cure together

✓ <u>Refrigeration tank:</u>
Climbs into a cold storage tank

✓ <u>Social Media Detox:</u>
Take a social media detox for a while

✓ <u>Fasting</u>
Fast together for a week

Eroticism:

Lapdance:
Performs a lap dance for the other person

Lingerie shopping:
Go lingerie shopping together

Rose petals bedroom:
Decorate your bedroom with rose petals

Role-playing games:
Role-playing games can bring a whole new experience into the relationship. Why not give it a try?

The more the better:
Try it in bed with several people

☑ Position cube
Buy a cube on which various positions are depicted

Swinger club:
Go to a swingers club

Bondage games:
Get tied up and see what your partner has planned for you.

BDSM:
Here goes a little further than bondage games...

Outdoors:

Find a nice place in nature where you have your dysentery...

✓ In the water:
It can also be a special experience in the water

✓ A short movie in front of it:
Watch a short movie beforehand and get in the mood

A short movie:
Shoot a little movie of yourselves

✓ Toys:
Try it with toys

✓ Kamasutra
Find inspiration in this special book

✓ Love swing:
A little acrobatic, but just as exciting

Alcohol:

Vineyard hike:
Take part in a vineyard hike

Wine tasting:
Take part in a wine tasting

Cocktail course:
Take part in a cocktail course

Whisky tasting:
Visit a whisky tasting

Cocktail recipe:
Create your own cocktail recipe

Pub crawl:
Take part in a pub crawl

Brewery tour:
Take part in a brewery tour

Gin tasting:
Visit a gin tasting

Oktoberfest:
Visit the Oktoberfest in Munich

Distill schnapps:
Distil your own schnapps

Motorsport experiences:

☑ Jet ski:
Ride on a jet ski

☑ Classic car:
Rent the classic car of your dreams

☑ Quad tour:
Take a quad bike tour on the beach

☑ Go-Kart:
Visit a go-kart track

☑ Snowmobile:
Ride on a snowmobile

☑ Off-road tour:
Go on an off-road tour with an off-road vehicle

☑ Race track:
Drive a racing car on a race track

☑ Motorcross:
Ride a motocross motorcycle on a hill track

☑ hovercraft:
Ride on a hovercraft

✓ Tanks:
Ride in a tank

Sporting events:

☑ **Boxing match:**
Watch a live professional boxing match.

☑ **Sumo wrestling:**
Watch a sumo fight

☑ **Ice hockey game:**
Attend an ice hockey game

☑ **Super Bowl:**
Watch the Super Bowl.

Wimbledon
Watch a Wimbledon match

☑ **Ski World Cup:**
Watch the Ski World Cup

☑ **Soccer World Cup**
Watch a game of the soccer World Cup

☑ **World Darts Championship**
Watch the World Darts Championship

☑ **US Masters Golf**
Visit the US Masters of Golf

✓ <u>Tour de France</u>
Watch the most important bicycle race in the world

✓ <u>NBA Finals</u>
Watch the NBA finals

Sports activities

☑ <u>Water skiing:</u>
Dare to get on the boards and go waterskiing

☑ <u>Personal Trainer:</u>
Let a personal trainer torture you for an hour

☑ <u>Jumphouse:</u>
Visit a jump house / trampoline park and feel weightless

☑ <u>Houserunning:</u>
Run along the wall of a house

☑ Bodyflying.
Bodyflying - overcoming gravity

☑ <u>High ropes course:</u>
Test your fear of heights in a high ropes course

☑ <u>Bicycle tour:</u>
Go on a bike tour together to an unknown location

☑ <u>Ice skating:</u>
Go ice skating on a frozen lake

☑ <u>Ski hall:</u>
Ride in a ski hall Ski

☑ **Zorbing:**

Feel spherical

☑ **Stand-up paddling:**

Keep your balance while stand-up paddling

☑ **Paraglider:**

Flies with a paraglider

☑ **Tough Mudder Event:**

Take part in a Tough Mudder event

☑ **Fitness Youtuber:**

Recreate the video of a fitness YouTuber together

☑ **Climbing hall:**

Go to a climbing gym

☑ **Marathon:**

Take part in a marathon and prepare together

☑ **Squash:**

Goes to play squash

☑ **Color Run:**

Take part in a Color Run

☑ **Martial arts:**

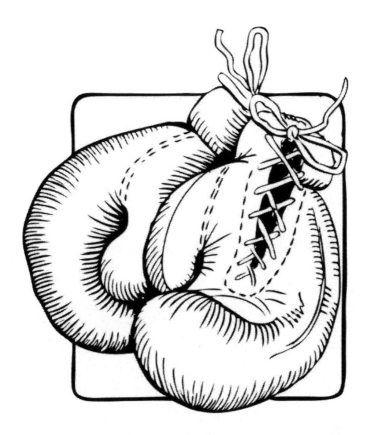

☑ **Tree climbing:**
Climb a tree together

☑ **Mechanical bull:**
Rides a mechanical bull

☑ **Jump sea cliff:**
Jumps off a cliff into the sea

☑ **Extreme hike:**
Take part in an extreme hike

☑ **<u>Blobbing:</u>**
Take off with blobbing

☑ **<u>Line Dance:</u>**
Take part in a line dance

☑ **<u>Tennis doubles:</u>**
Plays doubles tennis against another pair

☑ **<u>Tai Chi:</u>**
Take part in Tai Chi in the park

☑ **<u>Cricket:</u>**
Go play cricket together

☑ **<u>Tandem:</u>**
Ride on a tandem

Culture:

☑ __Variety:__
Visit a variety show

☑ __Theater:__
Go to a theater

☑ __City tour:__
Take part in a city tour in your own city

☑ __Ballet__
Attend a ballet together

☑ __Open Air Cinema:__
Visit an open-air movie theater

☑ __Art exhibition:__
Visit an art exhibition

☑ __Masked ball:__
Go to a masked ball together

☑ __Musical:__
Visit a famous musical

☑ __Travesty show:__
Visit a travesty show

☑ music festival:
Go to a music festival you don't know

☑ Vernissage:
Visit a vernissage together

☑ Opera:
Go to an opera

☑ Jazz concert:
Attend a jazz concert

☑ Poetry Slam:
Visit a poetry slam

☑ Knights' Festival:
Visit a knights' festival for a day

☑ **Rocky Horror Show:**
Visit the Rocky Horror Picture Show

☑ **Symphony concert:**
Attend a symphony concert

☑ **Wax museum:**
Visit a wax museum

☑ **Broadway show:**
Visit a Broadway show

☑ **Tropical house:**
Visit a tropical house

☑ **Fashion show:**
Visit a fashion show

☑ **Improvisational theater:**
Take part in improv theater

☑ **A bizarre museum:**
Visit a quirky museum

☑ **Holi Festival:**
Go to a Holi festival

☑ **Krampus run:**
Take part in a Krampus run

Relationship:

☑ **Bouquet of wild flowers:**
Present each other with a bouquet of wildflowers

☑ **Candlelight dinner:**
Visit a romantic candlelight dinner

☑ **Mistletoe:**
Kiss under a sprig of mistletoe

☑ **Underwater kiss:**
Kiss underwater and take a photo of it

☑ **Photo booth:**
Take crazy photos in a photo booth

☑ **Horoscope:**
Have your partner create a horoscope for you

☑ **3D photo shoot:**
Have your picture taken at a 3D photo shoot

☑ **Couple photo shoot:**
Do a couple photo shoot and hang up the best picture

☑ **Kiss the sea:**
Kiss in the sea

☑ <u>Double date:</u>
Goes on a double date with another couple

☑ <u>Partner Tattoo:</u>
Get a partner tattoo

☑ <u>Bed side exchange:</u>
Swap sides in bed for one night

☑ <u>Sand Initials:</u>
Write your initials in the sand

☑ <u>Concrete Initials:</u>
Write your initials in wet concrete

☑ <u>Waxing:</u>

Torture your partner during waxing

☑ <u>Truth or dare:</u>

Play Truth or Dare together

☑ <u>Golden wedding anniversary</u>

Celebrate your golden wedding anniversary together

☑ <u>First date:</u>

Repeat the first date

☑ <u>Starry sky kiss:</u>

Kiss each other under a clear starry sky

☑ <u>Drone selfie:</u>

Let a drone take off and photograph or film yourself

☑ <u>Partner look:</u>

Walk around in a partner look for a day

☑ <u>Luxury property:</u>

Get dressed up and view a luxury property

☑ <u>Couple matchmaking:</u>

Pairs up with another couple

☑ <u>Love letter:</u>

Write each other a love letter

☑ **Love lock:**

Attach a love lock to a bridge (Paris, Amsterdam, Cologne)

☑ **Waterfall kiss:**

Kiss under a waterfall

☑ **Shared tradition:**

Begins with a common tradition

☑ **Speed dating:**

Take part in a speed dating session and leave together

Further training and personal development:

☑ <u>New language:</u>
Learn a new language together

☑ <u>Dance course:</u>
Take part in a dance course (standard dance) including prom

☑ <u>Diving course:</u>
Take a diving course together

☑ <u>Salsa course:</u>
Take a salsa course together

☑ <u>Craft course:</u>
Attend a craft course together

☑ <u>Pottery course:</u>
Take a pottery course

☑ <u>Swimming badge:</u>
Do a swimming badge together

☑ <u>Sculptor course:</u>
Take a sculpture course

☑ **Surf course:**
Attend a surf course

☑ **Shooting training:**
Take part in shooting training

☑ **University lecture:**
Attends a university lecture

☑ **Salto**
Learn a somersault

☑ **Massage course:**
Attend a massage course together

☑ **Art course:**
Take part in an art course

✓ Goldsmith course:
Attends a goldsmithing course

✓ Kite surfing:
Let the wind take you and take a kitesurfing course

✓ Eat with chopsticks:
Learn to eat with chopsticks

✓ Spinning course:
Attend a spinning class together

✓ Nude painting course:
Attend a nude painting course

✓ Meditation workshop:
Take part in a meditation workshop

✓ Pole dance course:
Take part in a pole dance course

✓ New board game:
Learn a new board game

✓ Zumba course:
Attend a Zumba class

✓ Sign language:
Learns sign language

☑ <u>Reading:</u>
Attend the reading of a new book

☑ <u>Yoga course:</u>
Attend a yoga class

☑ <u>Driving safety:</u>
Completes a driver safety training course

☑ <u>DNA test:</u>
Take a DNA test

Culinary moments:

☑ Dark Dinner:
Visit a dark dinner

☑ Crime dinner:
Organize a murder mystery dinner together at your home

☑ Crime dinner 2:
Visit a murder mystery dinner away from home

☑ Make sushi:
Prepare your own sushi

☑ Praline course:
Take a chocolate course together

☑ Bad restaurant:
Visit the worst rated restaurant in your city

☑ Picking strawberries:
Go strawberry picking together and bake something with them

☑ Own ice cream:
Make your own ice cream

☑ <u>Erotic food cooking course:</u>
Take part in an erotic food cooking course

☑ <u>Knight's dinner:</u>
Take part in a knights' dinner

☑ <u>Make sausage:</u>
Make your own favorite sausage

☑ <u>Dinner in the Sky:</u>
Visit a "Dinner in the sky"

☑ <u>Barbecue course:</u>
Take a barbecue course

☑ <u>Mine dinner:</u>
Visit a mine dinner

☑ <u>Ice cream variety:</u>
Try an ice cream flavor you would never try

☑ <u>Gingerbread house:</u>
Bake your own gingerbread house

☑ <u>Weekly market:</u>
Go shopping together at a weekly market

☑ <u>1 star restaurant:</u>
Eat in a restaurant with at least 1 Michelin star

✓ **Stick bread:**
Bake your own bread on a stick

✓ **Own pasta:**
Make your own fresh pasta

✓ **Molecular cuisine:**
Try your hand at molecular cuisine

✓ **Vegan diet:**
Eat a vegetarian or vegan diet for 4 weeks

✓ **Scary dinner:**
Take part in a spooky dinner

☑ Cuban cigar:
Smoke a real Cuban cigar

☑ Restaurant order:
Stranger order - Ordered for the other person in the restaurant

☑ Truffle hunt:
Go on a truffle hunt (with or without pig/dog)

☑ Bake bread at home:
Bake your own bread at home

☑ Biggest sundae:
Order the biggest sundae on the menu

☑ Spiciest currywurst:
Eat the hottest currywurst there is

☑ Chocolate fondue:
Make your own chocolate fondue

☑ Running Dinner:
Take part in a running dinner

☑ Eating competition:
Take part in an eating competition

☑ Beekeeping honey:
Go beekeeping and make your own honey

☑ <u>Make macarons:</u>
Make your own macarons

☑ <u>Cow's milk:</u>
Milks a cow and drinks fresh milk

☑ <u>Insects:</u>
Eat deep-fried insects

☑ <u>3 courses 3 restaurants:</u>
Order 3 courses in 3 different restaurants in one evening

☑ <u>Cookies with initials:</u>
Bake cookies with your initials

☑ <u>Writing a cookbook:</u>
Create a cookbook together

☑ <u>Mouth robbery:</u>
Commits theft by mouth in a store

☑ <u>Breakfast in bed:</u>
Have breakfast in bed together

☑ <u>Family party:</u>
Organize a big family party and cook the food yourself

☑ <u>**Herb bed:**</u>

Create a herb bed and season your food with fresh herbs

Ententainment:

✅ <u>Paintball:</u>
Play paintball against each other

✅ <u>Drive-in movie:</u>
Visit a drive-in movie together

✅ <u>Virtual Reality:</u>
Visit a virtual reality experience

✅ <u>Labyrinth:</u>
Find your way out of a labyrinth together

✅ <u>Summer toboggan run:</u>
Ride down a summer toboggan run

✅ <u>Reality show:</u>
Apply for a reality show

✅ <u>Planetarium:</u>
Go to a planetarium

✅ <u>Moonlight Minigolf:</u>
Visit a Moonlight (3D/blacklight) minigolf course

✅ <u>Darts pub:</u>
Go to a darts pub and play darts

✓ **Pub Quiz:**
Win a pub quiz

✓ **Escape Room:**
Escape from an escape room

✓ **Karaoke bar:**
Sing a song together in a karaoke bar

✓ **Segway tour:**
Take a Segway tour

✓ **Roller skating party:**
Go to a roller skating party

✓ **Laser tag:**

Go play laser tag with friends

✓ **Geocaching:**
Take part in geocaching

✓ **Archery:**
Go archery together

✓ **Boccia:**
Plays boccia with pensioners in the park

✓ **Rickshaw:**
Ride in a rickshaw

✓ **Lost property auction:**
Take part in a lost property auction

✓ **E-scooter:**
Ride with an e-scooter

✓ **TV audience:**
Sit in the audience of your favorite TV show

✓ **Limousine:**
Hire a limousine and drive up to a party

✓ **Tupperware party:**
Take part in a Tupperware party

✓ **Harry Potter Marathon:**

Organize a Harry Potter Marathon

☑ <u>**Horror movie marathon at the cinema:**</u>
Visit a horror movie marathon at the cinema

☑ <u>**Host theme party:**</u>
Be the host of a theme party

☑ <u>**Favorite celebrities:**</u>
Meet your favorite celebrity

☑ <u>**Trade fair:**</u>
Visit a special trade fair

☑ <u>**Amusement park:**</u>
Go to an amusement park

Creativity:

☑ **Instagram trip:**
Faket a journey together on Instagram

☑ **Knitting:**
Knit your partner an item of clothing

☑ **Pumpkin carving:**
Carve a grimace out of a pumpkin

☑ **Amber stones:**
Collect amber on the beach and make something out of it

☑ **Flying kites:**
Fly a self-built kite

☑ **Youtube:**
Create your own YouTube channel

☑ **Own blog:**
Open your own blog

☑ **Furniture restoration:**
Enhances an old piece of furniture

☑ **Build furniture yourself:**
Build your own piece of furniture

☑ **Poem:**

Writes a poem to the other

☑ **Bullshit Bingo:**
Play Bullshit Bingo

☑ **Iris photo shoot:**
Do an iris photo shoot

☑ **Puzzle 1000 pieces:**
Puzzle together a puzzle with at least 1000 pieces

☑ **Photo album:**
Create a joint photo album

☑ **Draw a caricature:**
Have a street artist draw a caricature of you

☑ **Photowalk:**
Take part in a photo walk

☑ <u>CD burning:</u>
Burn a CD with your favorite music together

☑ <u>Origami folding:</u>
Try your hand at origami folding

☑ <u>Time capsule:</u>
Build your own time capsule

☑ <u>Bird house:</u>
Build your own birdhouse

☑ <u>Magic tricks:</u>
Learns magic tricks and shows them to the other person

☑ <u>Finger paints:</u>
Painting with finger paints

☑ <u>Monogram initial letters:</u>
Have a monogram designed from your initial letters

☑ <u>Song request radio:</u>
Wish for a song on the radio

☑ <u>Second hand store:</u>
Buy each other an outfit in the second-hand store

☑ **Couple's costume:**
Wear an eye-catching couple's costume for Halloween or carnival

☑ **House of cards restaurant:**
Builds a house of cards in the restaurant

☑ **Bodypainting:**
Paint each other in body painting

☑ **Model airplane:**
Build your own model airplane

☑ **Expand camper:**
Build an old camper according to your ideas

☑ **Flashmop:**
Take part in a flashmop

☑ **Balloon animals:**
Make your own balloon animals

☑ **Disposable camera:**
Documents an entire day with a disposable camera

Adventure:

☑ **Tree house:**
Spend a night together in a tree house

☑ **Snowshoe hike:**
Go on a snowshoe hike together

☑ **Rafting:**
Take part in a rafting tour

☑ **Sled dog ride:**
Take a dog sled ride

☑ **Wild waters:**
Floats down wild waters on an inflatable tire

☑ **Bungee jumping:**
Go bungee jumping together

☑ **Beach chair:**
Sleep a night in a beach chair

☑ **House by the lake**
Also rents an abandoned house by the lake with friends

☑ **Bootcamp:**
Survive a boot camp together

☑ <u>Inflatable boat tour:</u>
Go on an inflatable boat tour

☑ <u>Draisine:</u>
Ride on a trolley

☑ <u>Catamaran:</u>
Sailing towards the sun on a catamaran

☑ <u>Hot air balloon:</u>
Take a ride in a hot air balloon

☑ <u>Helicopter sightseeing flight:</u>
Take a helicopter tour

☑ <u>Stratospheric flight:</u>
Take a stratospheric flight
☑ <u>Nudist beach:</u>

Goes swimming at a nudist beach

☑ <u>Spend the night outdoors:</u>
Spend the night outdoors without a tent under the open sky

☑ <u>VW Bulli:</u>
Spends the night in a VW Bulli

☑ <u>Survival training:</u>
Attends a survival training course

☑ <u>Boat tour:</u>
Go on a boat tour with a motorboat

☑ <u>Night at the museum:</u>
Spend a night in the museum

☑ <u>High-rise roof:</u>
Try to get to the roof of a high-rise building and enjoy the view

☑ <u>Night bathing:</u>
Goes swimming secretly in a swimming pool at night

☑ <u>Zeppelin:</u>
Flies with a zeppelin airship

☑ <u>Night at the ghost hotel:</u>
Spend a night in a ghost hotel

☑ <u>Dolphins:</u>
Swims with dolphins

☑ <u>Lost Place:</u>
Visit a lost place

☑ <u>Night hike in the forest:</u>
Take a night hike through the forest

☑ <u>Shark cage:</u>
Dive in a cage with sharks

☑ <u>Aerobatic airplane</u>
Flies as co-pilot in an aerobatic airplane.

☑ <u>Parachute</u>
Do a parachute jump

☑ <u>Cave tour:</u>
Visit a cave

☑ <u>Igloo:</u>
Spend a night in an igloo

Travel:

☑ <u>Alpaca hike:</u>
Take part in an alpaca hike

☑ <u>Sailing trip:</u>
Go on a romantic sailing trip

☑ <u>San Francisco:</u>
Walk like a hippy through San Francisco for once

☑ <u>Canoe tour:</u>
Go on a canoe tour

☑ <u>Disneyland:</u>
Take a trip to Disneyland

☑ <u>7 Summits:</u>
Climb one of the 7 summits together

☑ <u>Taj Mahal:</u>
Swear eternal love in front of the Taj Mahal

☑ <u>Active vacation:</u>
Go on an active vacation (e.g. hiking, surfing)

☑ <u>Backpacking trip:</u>
Pack your bags and go on a backpacking trip

☑ **Business class flight**

Treat yourself to a Business Class flight on a long-haul trip

☑ **Castle Overnight stay:**

Spend a night in a castle

☑ **Mountain hut:**

Rent a romantic mountain hut

☑ **Wine barrel overnight stay:**

Spends the night in a wine barrel

☑ **Palm Island Dubai:**

Visit the Palm Island in Dubai

☑ **Donkey hiking tour:**

Go on a hiking tour with donkeys

☑ **Cologne Cathedral:**

Visit Cologne Cathedral

☑ **Dream vacation:**

Enjoy a dream vacation with your own water bungalow

☑ **Favorite film locations:**

Visit the filming locations of your favorite series/movie

☑ **Romantic hotel:**

Spend a weekend in a romantic hotel

☑ <u>Route 66</u>
Drive along the most famous road in the USA

☑ <u>Spitsbergen:</u>
Explore the wilderness in Spitsbergen

☑ <u>Rail cruise:</u>
Take a rail cruise in a special country

☑ <u>Honeymoon Maldives:</u>
Spend your honeymoon in the Maldives

☑ <u>New York:</u>
Travel to New York and visit the Statue of Liberty

☑ <u>Heligoland:</u>
Travel to Heligoland and eat a fresh fish sandwich

☑ <u>Glamping:</u>
Spend a weekend glamping

☑ <u>First class train:</u>
Travel in the first class of a train

☑ <u>New Year's Eve abroad:</u>
Celebrate New Year's Eve abroad

☑ **7 wonders of the world:**
Visit each of the 7 wonders of the world

☑ **Cabin Sweden:**
Spends two weeks in a lonely wooden hut in Sweden

☑ **Ice hotel:**
Spend a night in an ice hotel

☑ **Jungle tour:**
Go on a jungle tour with a guide

☑ **Couchsurfing:**
Power of couchsurfing in a foreign city

☑ **Host couchsurfers:**
Take a couchsurfer into your home

☑ **Airport surprise:**
Drive to the airport and get on the first plane. You'll be surprised where it takes you

☑ **Road trip USA:**
Take a road trip through the USA

☑ **Embrace the sequoia:**
Hug a sequoia tree together

☑ **World map with pins:**

Hang up a world map with pins

☑ <u>Orient Express:</u>
Ride on the Orient Express

☑ <u>Cooking course abroad:</u>
Take part in a cooking course in another country

☑ <u>Whale Watching:</u>
Take part in a whale watching tour

☑ <u>Northern Lights:</u>
Marvel at the northern lights

☑ <u>Night in the tepee:</u>
Spend a night in a tipi

☑ <u>Drink coconut:</u>
Look for a coconut on vacation and drink from it

☑ <u>Carnival Rio:</u>
Celebrate the world's most famous carnival in Rio de Janeiro

☑ <u>Vespa Rome:</u>
Ride through Rome on a Vespa

☑ <u>Venice gondola ride:</u>
Book a gondola ride through Venice

☑ **Safari in Africa:**
Take part in a safari in Africa

☑ **Camping:**
Go camping

☑ **Tour de France:**
Watch the Tour de France live at the racecourse

☑ **Bubble Hotel:**
Spend the night in a bubble hotel

☑ **Cherry Blossom Festival Japan:**
Admire the cherry blossom festival in Japan

☑ **Hotel own city:**
Spend the night in a hotel in your own city

☑ **Kiss Eiffel Tower:**
Kiss on the Eiffel Tower

☑ **Lighthouse overnight stay:**
Spend the night in a lighthouse

☑ **Austria Romatikstraße:**
Take a road trip on the Austrian Romantic Road

☑ **Christmas in the snow:**
Spend Christmas in the snow

☑️ <u>Lonely island:</u>
Spend the night on a desert island

☑️ <u>Yodeling:</u>
Go yodeling in the mountains

☑️ <u>Romeo and Juliet:</u>
Visit the locations of Shakespeare's Romeo and Juliet

☑️ <u>Indian Summer:</u>
Experience the Indian summer in New England

☑️ <u>Bullfighting:</u>
Watch a bullfight in Spain

☑️ <u>Sleeperoo Cube:</u>
Spend a night in a Sleeperoo Cube

☑️ <u>Black beach:</u>
Go for a walk on a beach with black sand

☑️ <u>Pink beach:</u>
Go for a walk on a beach with pink sand
☑️ <u>Houseboat:</u>
Spend your vacation in a houseboat

☑️ <u>Room Service:</u>
Let the room service in the hotel serve you for 1 day.

☑️ <u>Wellness Suite:</u>

Book a private wellness suite

☑ **Dead Sea:**
Go swimming in the Dead Sea

☑ **Stay abroad:**
Lives abroad for a few months

☑ **Cocktail Hawaii:**
Sip a cocktail in Hawaii

☑ **Plan a trip around the world:**
Plan a trip around the world together

☑ **Way of St. James:**
Walk along the Way of St. James

☑ **Spontaneous road trip:**
Start a spontaneous road trip

☑ **Volcano:**
Visit an active volcano

☑ **Pope:**
Listen to the Pope speak in the Vatican

☑ **La Tomatina:**
Take part in La Tomatina in Spain

☑ **GP Monaco:**

Watch the Monaco Grand Prix at the racetrack

☑ **Catacombs Paris:**
Visit the catacombs of Paris

☑ **Blind booking:**
Try your luck at blind booking

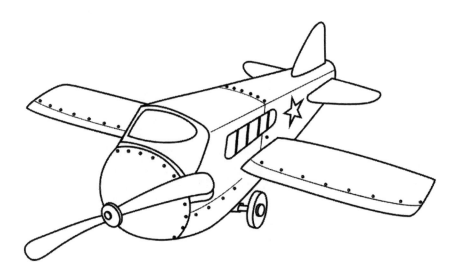

Your own bucket list

And now it's your turn :

On the following pages you now have the opportunity to compile your own bucket lists.

Whether you want to put together your most interesting experiences from a single category or a mix of different categories, e.g. for an exciting weekend, a planned short trip or a week's vacation at home, is up to you.

Another option, of course, is for each partner to put together their own bucket list of experiences that they would definitely like to experience with their partner. As we know, tastes are different. So the woman goes motorcrossing and the man takes a salsa course together. And maybe you'll find completely new common interests :)

Give free rein to your creativity and always ensure a certain amount of variety.

Our bucket list for:

....

☐	
☐	
☐	
☐	
☐	
☐	
☐	
☐	

Our bucket list for:

....

☐	
☐	
☐	
☐	
☐	
☐	
☐	
☐	

Our bucket list for:

....

☐	
☐	
☐	
☐	
☐	
☐	
☐	
☐	

Our bucket list for:

....

☐	
☐	
☐	
☐	
☐	
☐	
☐	
☐	

Our bucket list for:

....

☐	
☐	
☐	
☐	
☐	
☐	
☐	
☐	

Our bucket list for:

....

☐	
☐	
☐	
☐	
☐	
☐	
☐	
☐	

Our bucket list for:

....

☐	
☐	
☐	
☐	
☐	
☐	
☐	
☐	

Our bucket list for:

....

☐	
☐	
☐	
☐	
☐	
☐	
☐	
☐	

Our bucket list for:

....

☐	
☐	
☐	
☐	
☐	
☐	
☐	
☐	

Our bucket list for:

....

☐	
☐	
☐	
☐	
☐	
☐	
☐	
☐	

Photo album:

Special experiences always result in unique pictures. And as we know. A picture tells more than 1000 words.

Here you have the opportunity to record these pictures and stick them in. This way you know exactly where to find them and they certainly can't get lost.

Whether you take a single picture for each experience or fill an entire page with a very special experience is of course up to you.

A little tip: It's a good idea to have a Polaroid camera with you on your adventures so that you really only take one photo at a special moment and the photo can be glued in perfectly :)

Our most beautiful photo album:

Our most beautiful photo album:

Our most beautiful photo album:

Our most beautiful photo album:

Our most beautiful photo album:

Our most beautiful photo album:

Our most beautiful photo album:

Our most beautiful photo album:

Our most beautiful photo album:

Our most beautiful photo album:

Closing words:

In the paperback version, you would now have the opportunity to write your own bucket list on pre-printed pages. You can also stick your best experiences into the book as photos in Polaroid format. However, this was deliberately left out of the ebook version, as it wouldn't make sense to write something on your screen or stick photos on it :D

I hope this book has given you some inspiration and that you've already had some wonderful experiences with it. I hope even more that many more special experiences will follow during your relationship and that this book can support you :)

Printed in Great Britain
by Amazon

53840204R00051